"...Robin M. Donovan weaves a classic tale with a modern twist that engages the imagination and warms the spirit... Through descriptive and captivating imagery, Christmas Village comes alive, and Snowflake and Snowbell's courageous journey reminds us to be grateful for our blessings. Whether you are a child or a child at heart, readers of all ages will... enjoy this inspiring and heartwarming adventure..."

—Melissa Dawn Reedy,
author of *A Westward Adventure Series*

A Christmas Rescue

A Christmas Rescue

by Robin Michelle Donovan

Published by Tate Publishing & Enterprises, LLC
127 E. Trade Center Terrace | Mustang, Oklahoma 73064 USA
1.888.361.9473 | www.tatepublishing.com

Tate Publishing is committed to excellence in the publishing industry. The company reflects the philosophy established by the founders, based on Psalm 68:11,
"The Lord gave the word and great was the company of those who published it."

Cover and interior design by Elizabeth M. Hawkins
Illustrations by Brandon Wood

Published in the United States of America

ISBN: 978-1-61346-439-7
1. Juvenile Fiction / General
2. Juvenile Fiction / Holidays & Celebrations / Christmas & Advent
11.08.24

Dedication

This book is dedicated to my family for all their support, guidance, encouragement, and most importantly love.

Patricia Reedy
John Reedy
Melissa Reedy
Adrian Donovan
Billy Donovan
Tulane Donovan
Shaun Donovan
Robbie Brown
Harry Brown, Jr.

They have taught me that family and being close to the ones you love is what gives you wings to reach the stars. They have also given me comfort knowing that even if my wings fail, they will be there to dust me off and encourage me to try again.

This book is also in memory of my grandparents Robbie and Harry Brown and mother-in-law Tulane Donovan. Their wonderful impact on my life is immeasurable. They will never be forgotten.

In particular, this story is dedicated to my mom, Patricia Reedy, and my sister, Melissa Reedy, because it was originally a Christmas present to them. The characters Snowflake and Snowbell were based on my sister and me, and Fiona, the cub's mother, was based on my mom.

Table of Contents

The Sisters Meet an Elf	11
Christmas Village	19
Kidnapped	29
The Search Begins	41
The Prisoners Meet	51
The Rescue	61
A Gift from the Heart	69
Christmas Is Saved	77

The Sisters Meet an Elf

Long, long ago near the North Pole, two young polar bears were wandering over the ice and snow. Each polar bear had on a red scarf and looked identical, except that one had a snowflake birthmark on her hip. The two polar bears were weary and tired-out from searching in the snow, so they decided to rest for a while. Suddenly, they saw bright headlights from a vehicle coming at them from a few yards away.

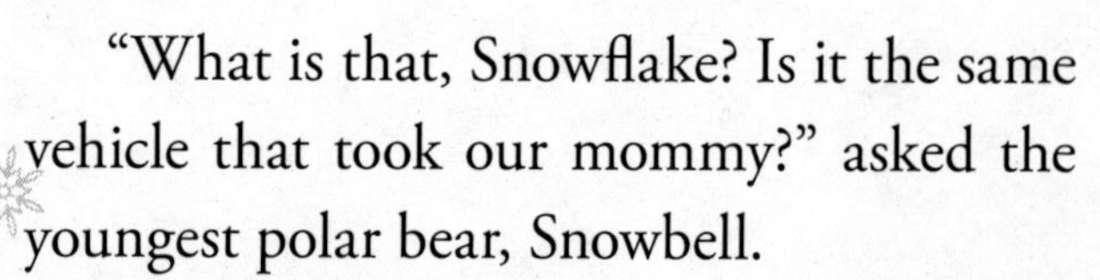

“What is that, Snowflake? Is it the same vehicle that took our mommy?” asked the youngest polar bear, Snowbell.

“No, Snowbell, those were much larger headlights. And anyway, I won’t let anything happen to you. I promised Mommy, remember, and you know I won’t go back on my promise to her. Come on, Snowbell, let’s go hide behind that hill over there until it passes by,” Snowflake said.

As the two polar bears headed for the hill, Snowbell’s scarf came off.

“I’ve got to get my scarf!” Snowbell said.

Snowflake ran and jumped in front of her little sister. “Snowbell, you can’t go and get it. We don’t know who is driving the vehicle.”

“I have to go get it, Snowflake. Mommy gave us our scarves, and now she is gone. It’s the only thing I have that reminds me of

her." Snowbell looked up at her sister with tears in her eyes.

"First of all, Mom is not gone. We will find her. Until then, I'll go get your scarf, and no matter what happens, stay here, okay?" The lights got closer as Snowflake headed for the scarf lying in the snow. She reached down and carefully picked up the scarf with her mouth. She was glad that Mom had given these scarves to her and her sister as early Christmas presents. She didn't know what she'd do without her scarf to give her courage to take care of her sister, because all she wanted to do was cry. She looked up and saw the lights were close. She could make out the type of vehicle, and she could see the silhouette of the driver. It was a snowmobile-type vehicle pulling a trailer behind it. The driver was small, much smaller than the humans that took her mother.

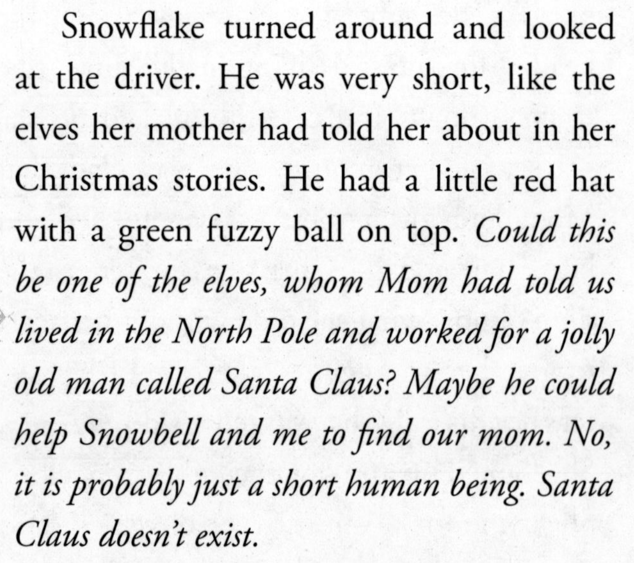

Snowflake was about to join her sister behind the hill when the driver called out, "Hey there. You're pretty young to be out here without your mother. Is she around here somewhere?"

Snowflake turned around and looked at the driver. He was very short, like the elves her mother had told her about in her Christmas stories. He had a little red hat with a green fuzzy ball on top. *Could this be one of the elves, whom Mom had told us lived in the North Pole and worked for a jolly old man called Santa Claus? Maybe he could help Snowbell and me to find our mom. No, it is probably just a short human being. Santa Claus doesn't exist.*

"Little polar bear, are you okay? I'm not going to hurt you. I just want to know if there is anything I can do. The boss would be very upset with me if I neglected to help anyone who may need it."

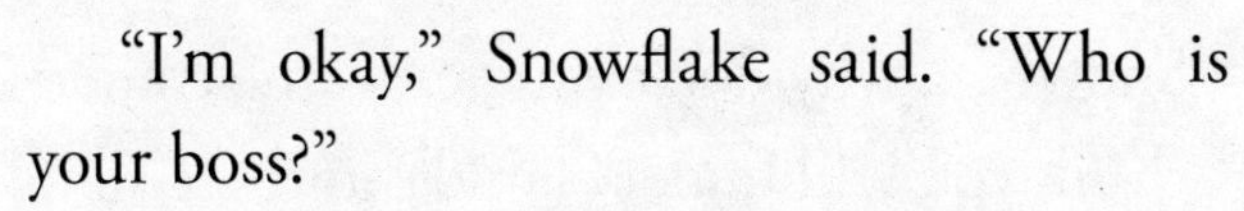

"I'm okay," Snowflake said. "Who is your boss?"

"Santa Claus, of course. My name is Jingle. What's yours?"

"My name is Snowflake," said the young polar bear. She turned to call her sister who came bounding up. "This energetic little ball of white fur is my little sister, Snowbell. Snowbell, this is Jingle."

"Snowflake, you found an elf!" Snowbell said. She looked up at the elf with hopeful eyes. "Sir, do you know Santa? I need to ask him to help me and my sister find our mom."

"Yes, I know Santa. In fact, I work for him. Now I don't know if Santa can help your mother, but I'm sure he will do his best. Why don't we get you to Santa's house, and you two can tell him about your mother. Both of you can also get something to eat and some sleep. You look pretty worn out.

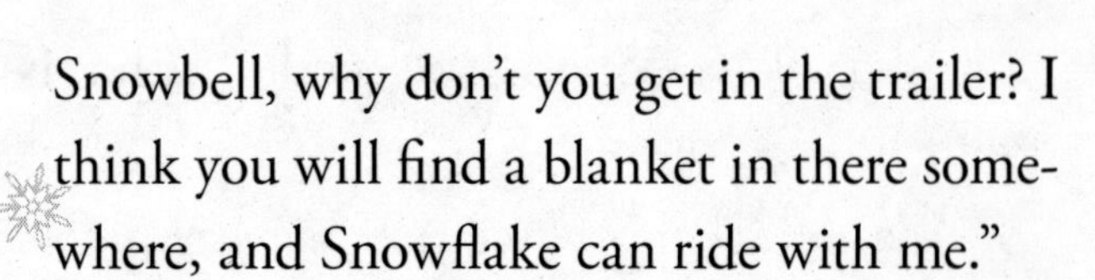

Snowbell, why don't you get in the trailer? I think you will find a blanket in there somewhere, and Snowflake can ride with me."

Snowbell jumped in the trailer and yawned. "I am pretty tired. Snowflake, will you wake me when we get there?"

"Of course I will. Now go to sleep, and sweet dreams." Snowflake gave her sister a kiss on the nose.

Snowflake then jumped up into the seat beside Jingle. "Do you really think that your boss, whoever he is, can help us find our mom?" She was still not sure that the Santa Claus of her mother's stories was real, even though her sister thought he was.

"I know that if it is possible for your mother to be saved, Santa is the one to do it. Now, why don't you get some sleep? We have a long way to go," Jingle said.

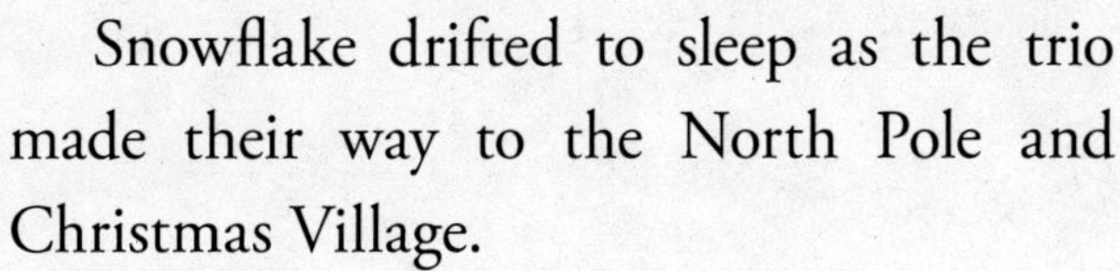

Snowflake drifted to sleep as the trio made their way to the North Pole and Christmas Village.

Christmas Village

"Snowflake, Snowflake, wake up! We're almost there," Jingle said, nudging the young polar bear.

As Snowflake came out of her deep sleep, she realized that the vehicle had stopped moving. She opened her eyes and looked around. All she saw was a tall pole. It was white, with green and white stripes, and had a sign on it that said, "North Pole." On

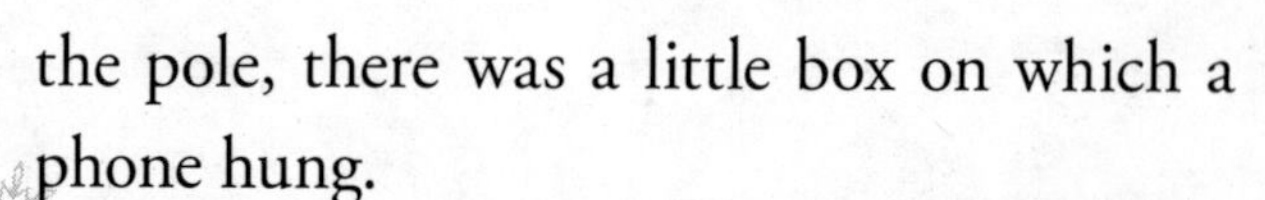

the pole, there was a little box on which a phone hung.

"Christmas Village is right over that hill. I thought you and Snowbell might want the full experience of seeing it from far away," Jingle said. "Now, go wake your sister, and I'll go let them know we are coming, so they can turn off the cloaking device."

"Jingle, what's a cloaking device?" Snowflake asked as Jingle paused before getting out of the vehicle.

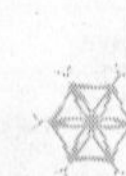

"In order to keep the location of Christmas Village a secret, the elves came up with a cloaking device. It's a device that makes Christmas Village invisible and protects it from attack," explained Jingle as he got out of the jeep and walked to the phone on the pole.

While Jingle was talking to the command operator at Christmas Village,

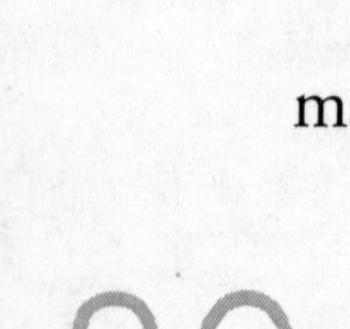

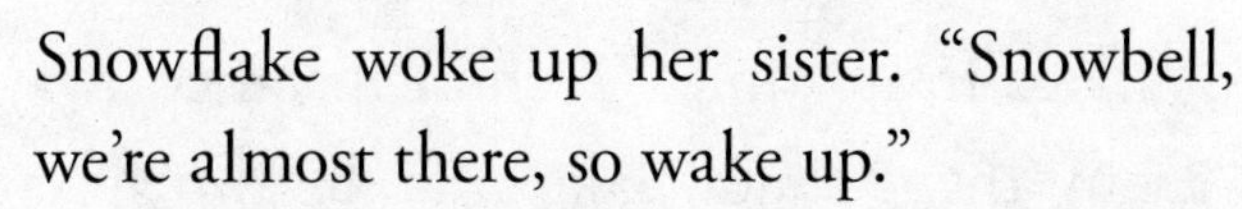

Snowflake woke up her sister. “Snowbell, we’re almost there, so wake up.”

Snowbell opened her eyes, and her face lit up as she saw the North Pole. “It’s the North Pole, like in Mommy’s stories!”

Jingle returned and said, “I told them to get a message to Santa that he will have two visitors. I also asked them to wait for a while before they turn off the device, because it is the most beautiful sight, and I want the two of you to see it up close. Now, let’s get a move on.”

Jingle jumped back in his vehicle, turned the ignition on, and in no time they were once again on their way. As they dashed over the hill, they expected to see an immense village, but saw nothing except more snow and hills. Jingle went a little farther and stopped.

“I know it looks barren now, but just look that way, and you will see Christmas

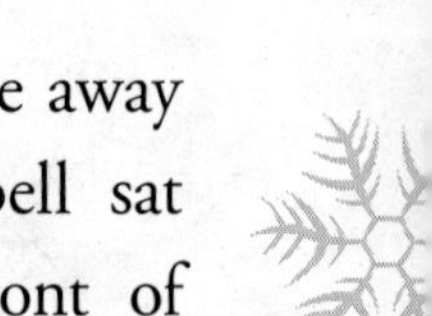

Village in no time." A short distance away from them, Snowflake and Snowbell sat in amazement because right in front of them was what looked like a floating, see-through curtain. There were so many colors. Snowflake remembered the northern lights that their mother had shown them a few years ago, and this was definitely far prettier. There were pinks, purples, yellows, blues, and so many other colors she didn't even recognize. Then suddenly, she could see the village that was slowly beginning to appear as the colors began to fade. The village was beautiful. There were so many houses, and they could see hundreds of elves running around busily. The vehicle began to move. As they got closer, Snowflake saw that there was a gate blocking the path leading into the Village. It was made of gold, and on part of the gate was a design. The more Snowflake looked, the more she

realized that the design was of Santa and eight reindeer pulling a sleigh. As they got closer, Jingle slowed down and stopped in front. Then with a wave of Jingle's hand, and a little elf magic, the gate mysteriously opened.

Maybe Mom was right about all this Santa Claus stuff, Snowflake thought. She glanced over at Snowbell, whose eyes were wide open, and she had a great big smile on her face.

Jingle drove the car through the gates and down the path into the village. Each building had a sign on it, such as "Doll Workshop," "Music Center," and "Computerized Department." Jingle continued to drive toward a huge house, much bigger than all the rest. It also had a stable next to it, and some of the reindeer were outside exercising. Jingle parked the vehicle right outside the door and jumped

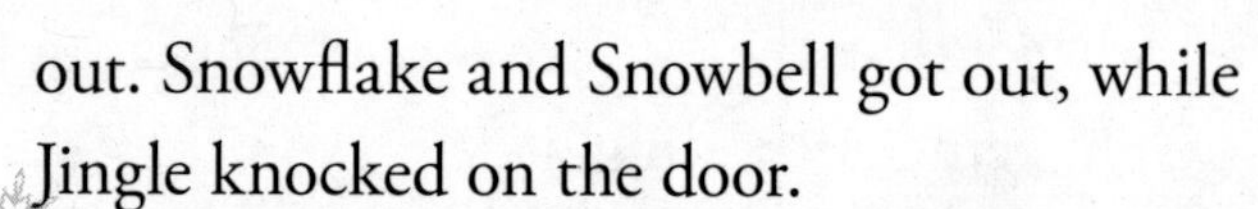

out. Snowflake and Snowbell got out, while Jingle knocked on the door.

As the door opened, Snowflake saw another elf wearing a blue hat with a yellow fuzzy ball on top.

"Come in! We have been expecting you. Santa thought it best for both of you to get a good meal and some sleep. He is on an inspection of the teddy bear workshop and will see you later. I'm Tinsel. If I can help you in any way, let me know. Now follow me, and I'll show you to your room. Ginger, our cook, will have a meal whipped up in no time. By the time you clean up and come back down, she'll have everything ready."

The smell of chocolate chip cookies wafted to Snowflake's keen nose as she walked into the front room. She remembered the wonderful cookies that her mother would always make this time of year. How

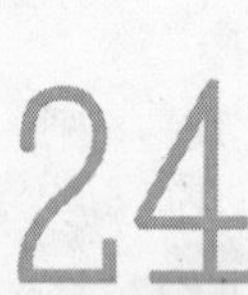

she missed her. She hoped this guy Santa, whoever he was, could help.

Snowflake was led past a huge room, which she glanced in as she went past. It had two big comfy easy chairs beside a huge fireplace in which a warm fire blazed. She continued to follow Tinsel as he led her and her sister to a flight of stairs. The whole house was decorated for Christmas with lights, holly, and tinsel everywhere. They were led up the stairs to a room. Tinsel opened the door and gestured for Snowflake and Snowbell to go on in. The room was large, with a huge bed in the middle of the room. "This is for you, Snowflake. The adjoining room will be Snowbell's, which can be reached through this door. When you finish, come down stairs, and Ginger will have your meal prepared," Tinsel said. Tinsel left, leaving the two sisters to get used to their surroundings.

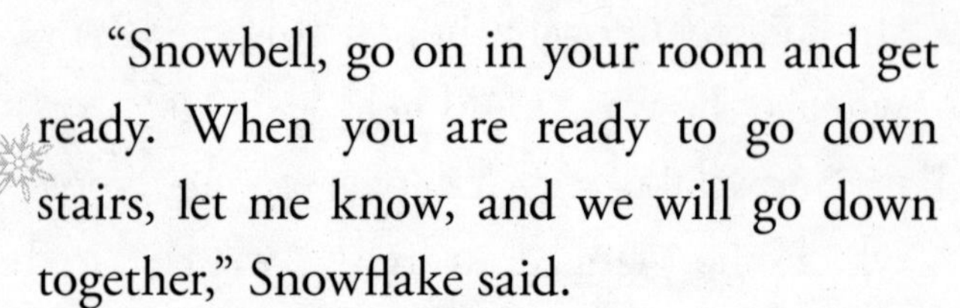

"Snowbell, go on in your room and get ready. When you are ready to go down stairs, let me know, and we will go down together," Snowflake said.

"Okay, but could you leave the door open?" Snowbell was a little afraid of being in a strange place.

"Don't worry. I will. Now go on and get ready," said Snowflake.

Snowbell went into her room as Snowflake made a closer inspection of the room. There was a window beside the bed, and she went over to it and looked out. The view was of more buildings that were behind the house. They were little buildings for the elves, she assumed. Soon Snowbell came in, and they headed downstairs.

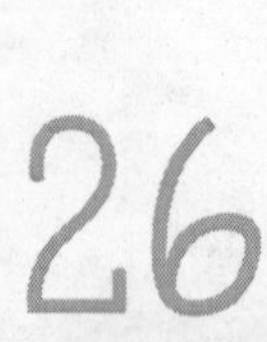

MR.
MRS.

Kidnapped

When Snowflake and Snowbell got to the bottom of the stairs, their noses picked up wonderful fragrances coming from the kitchen. The two polar bears cautiously headed toward the kitchen. Snowflake peeked around the door, her little black nose taking in all the smells. She smelled the wonderful aroma of chocolate chip cookies, pumpkin pies, and ham. Snowflake saw a female elf. She had light tan hair and wore an apron, tied around her little waist.

She turned around and looked directly at Snowflake with a great big smile on her face.

"Come on in. You must be Snowflake and Snowbell. I'm Ginger. Jingle told me a lot about you. He said the two of you are all alone and are trying to find your mom."

"Yes, we were hoping that Santa could help. It would be the best present in the world to have our whole family back together again. If anyone can do it, I know Santa can," Snowbell said.

"Well, don't you worry. Santa is due here any time now. Why don't you go into the other room and sit by the fire. We'll have dinner in a few minutes. I believe that Jingle is in the other room. You could ask him to tell you a story."

"Cool!" Snowbell said, running into the other room and sitting on the floor near Jingle. Snowflake turned around and headed into the other room as well. Jingle told them

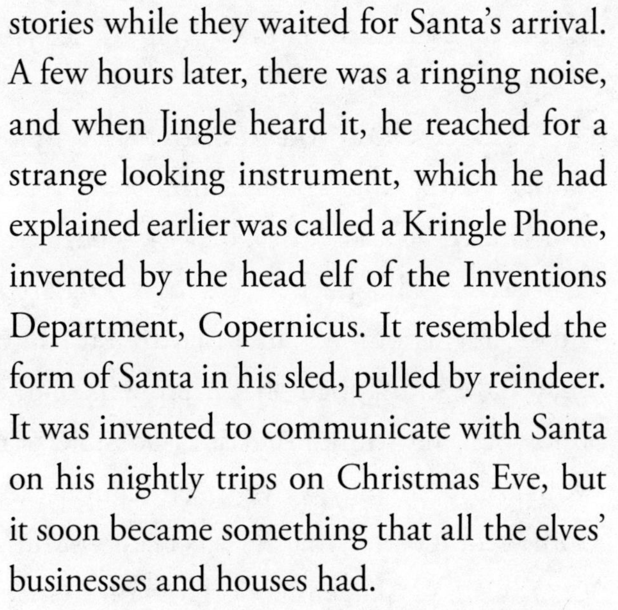

stories while they waited for Santa's arrival. A few hours later, there was a ringing noise, and when Jingle heard it, he reached for a strange looking instrument, which he had explained earlier was called a Kringle Phone, invented by the head elf of the Inventions Department, Copernicus. It resembled the form of Santa in his sled, pulled by reindeer. It was invented to communicate with Santa on his nightly trips on Christmas Eve, but it soon became something that all the elves' businesses and houses had.

"Hello?" Jingle answered. "Are you sure? Okay, I'll get a group together and meet you there… Hey, Caska! Could these be the same people who took the two polar bears' mother? Okay, I'll bring them with me, and we'll see… I know. I hope it isn't Frostbite either. He hasn't done anything since the last time we thwarted his scheme. I hope he

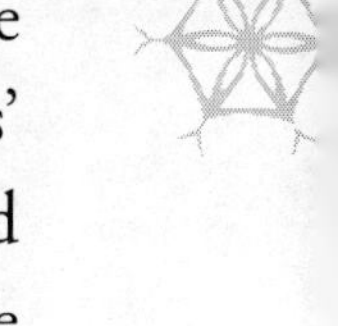

hasn't devised another one. Well, I'll see you soon.

"Ginger, could you come in here?" Jingle said. "Santa and the reindeer have been kidnapped. Caska, the chief of security at Christmas Village, believes that Frederick Frostbite, whom we all just call Frostbite, may have kidnapped them. Snowflake and Snowbell, he thinks that it is possible that your mother may have been caught for some strange plot that he has been working on as well. Caska wants both of you to meet him, and hopefully, if you tell him what happened to your mom, he could figure out something that could help us find your mother, Santa, and the reindeer."

"We'd be glad to help in any way we can," Snowflake said.

"Ginger, could you put together a bag of food that we could take with us?" Jingle asked.

"Of course, I'll put together something right now."

Jingle then picked up the phone and dialed the number for the reindeer stables. "Hello, Farley. Did you hear about Santa and the reindeer being kidnapped? You did! Well, I was wondering if you have any reindeer in the stables that were not out in the field. We need them to help us get to the location where Santa and the reindeer were kidnapped."

"A few, mainly the second string ones, and Prancer and Blitzen are here. They were both nursing a pulled muscle. I was going to let them out into the field tomorrow. I could harness them to the smaller sleds."

"That is good. I'll be there soon. Oh! Farley, don't worry. I know how much you care for those reindeer, and I'll make sure we get them back to you, safe and sound." Jingle hung up the phone and dialed again.

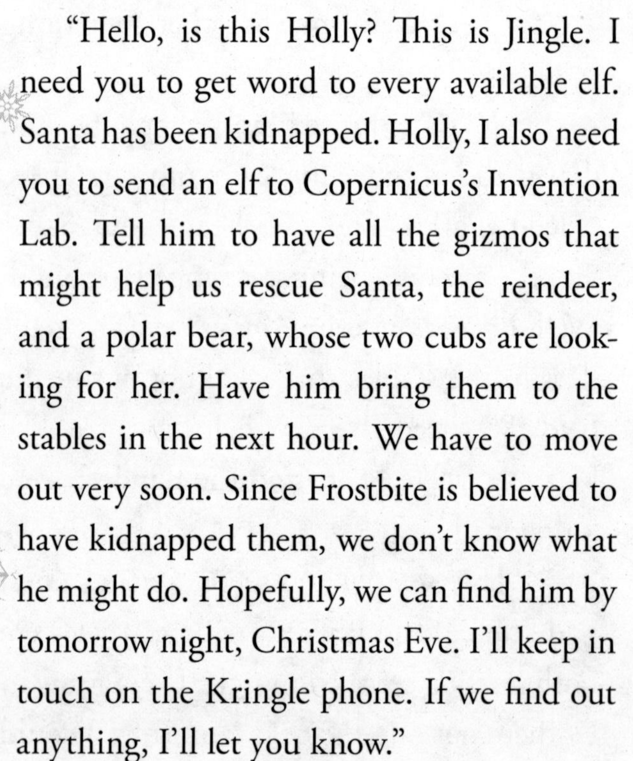

"Hello, is this Holly? This is Jingle. I need you to get word to every available elf. Santa has been kidnapped. Holly, I also need you to send an elf to Copernicus's Invention Lab. Tell him to have all the gizmos that might help us rescue Santa, the reindeer, and a polar bear, whose two cubs are looking for her. Have him bring them to the stables in the next hour. We have to move out very soon. Since Frostbite is believed to have kidnapped them, we don't know what he might do. Hopefully, we can find him by tomorrow night, Christmas Eve. I'll keep in touch on the Kringle phone. If we find out anything, I'll let you know."

Jingle then rushed Snowflake and Snowbell out of the house and over to the reindeer stables, grabbing the bag of food that Ginger gave him on the way. In no time, a lightweight sled was readied for takeoff as five relatively inexperienced reindeer and

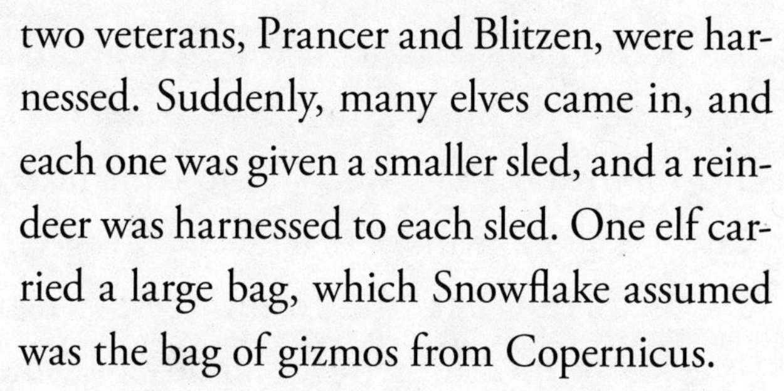

two veterans, Prancer and Blitzen, were harnessed. Suddenly, many elves came in, and each one was given a smaller sled, and a reindeer was harnessed to each sled. One elf carried a large bag, which Snowflake assumed was the bag of gizmos from Copernicus.

"Well, Jingle those are all the reindeer I have who are at least somewhat experienced with pulling a sled," Farley said.

Jingle chose to drive the larger sled, which was just big enough for two young polar bears and an elf. The bottom of the sled was covered with hay. "Snowflake and Snowbell, why don't you two get into the sleigh, while I say a few more things to the elves?" Jingle said.

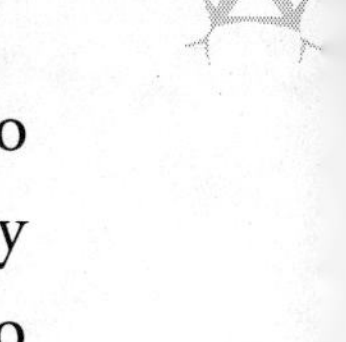

Snowflake and Snowbell jumped into the sleigh. They decided to lie in the hay while they were waiting for Jingle and try to get some sleep. Snowflake breathed in the warm, sweet scent of hay. It reminded her of

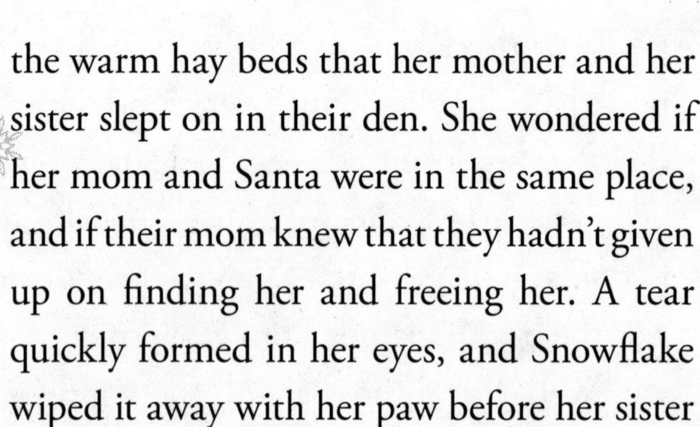

the warm hay beds that her mother and her sister slept on in their den. She wondered if her mom and Santa were in the same place, and if their mom knew that they hadn't given up on finding her and freeing her. A tear quickly formed in her eyes, and Snowflake wiped it away with her paw before her sister could see. What if they never found their mom or Santa and the reindeer? Christmas wouldn't exist anymore, and she would have to find a way to take care of her sister all by herself.

"Don't worry, sis. Santa will take care of Mom until we find her. And the elves will find her, because remember, they have elf magic," Snowbell said.

"Thank you, Snowbell. I needed you to remind me to be optimistic. You always know when something is wrong. I just wish I could have stopped them from taking her. If I could have just been bigger, or jumped

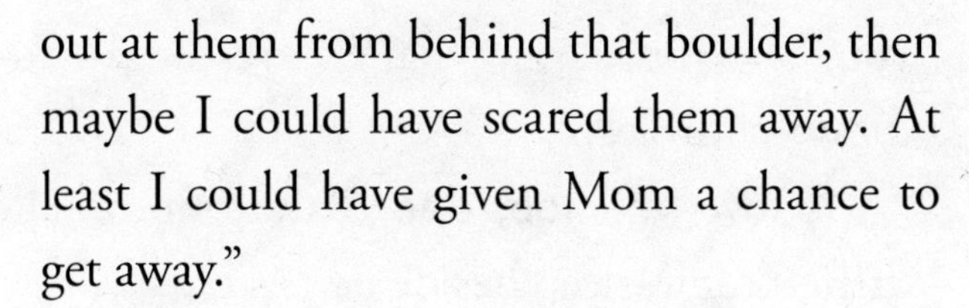

out at them from behind that boulder, then maybe I could have scared them away. At least I could have given Mom a chance to get away."

"I'm glad you didn't do anything. If you had, then you could have been caught, and I could not have made it this far if you had not been here for me. I was about to give up when that blizzard hit. You wouldn't let me, and you even helped me when I got too tired to go on. So don't say that you didn't do anything to help Mom, because I know she feels much better knowing that we have each other and aren't all alone."

"Thank you, Snowbell. I'm glad you are here too, because when I run out of hope and optimism, or feel like I'm all alone, then I just look at you, and I know that I'm not alone. I know that I have something that is better than anything else in the world. I have a sister, who loves me very much. I love

you, Snowbell." Snowflake's eyes began to droop with sleep.

"I love you too, Snowflake." Snowbell drifted off to sleep beside her sister.

Snowflake placed her front leg over her sister. "I won't let you down, sis. One way or another, I will find our mom and reunite our family for Christmas." The two polar bears were still asleep when Jingle and the other elves were preparing for takeoff. Jingle decided they should rest and that he would wake them when they got to Caska's location. The reindeer and sleds were led out of the stable, and into the takeoff field that ended in a cliff. The reindeer began to run, and as they reached the cliff, they took off into the sky.

HQ

The Search Begins

The elves and sleighs had landed at Caska's designated spot, and the elves were now discussing plans for a search of the area, to see if Santa, the reindeer, or the two polar bears' mother could be found by air. Jingle was looking for Caska and finally found him giving instructions to his security elf. After the security elf left, Jingle asked, "Hey, Caska, have you been able to get any leads?"

"Oh! Hi, Jingle. I have gotten a few

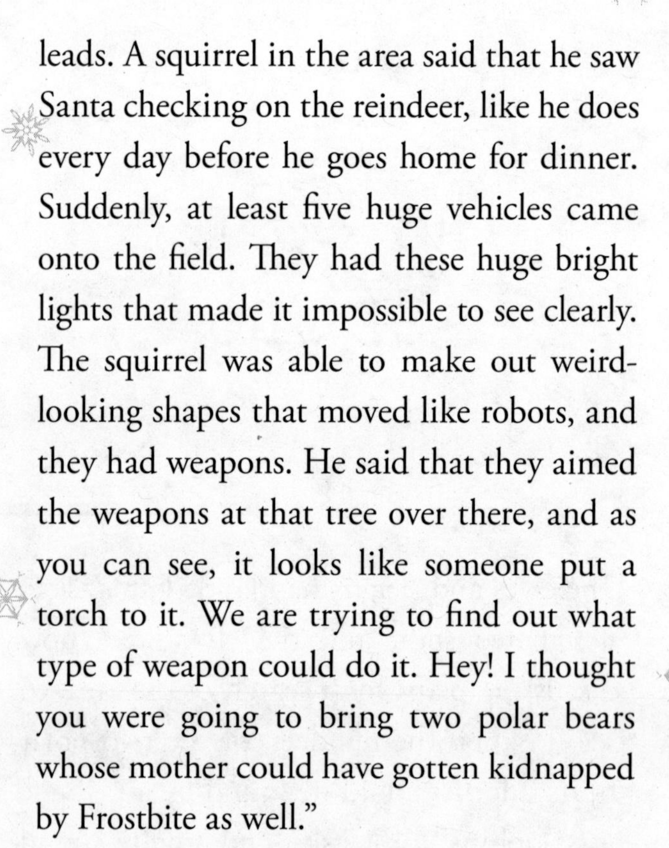

leads. A squirrel in the area said that he saw Santa checking on the reindeer, like he does every day before he goes home for dinner. Suddenly, at least five huge vehicles came onto the field. They had these huge bright lights that made it impossible to see clearly. The squirrel was able to make out weird-looking shapes that moved like robots, and they had weapons. He said that they aimed the weapons at that tree over there, and as you can see, it looks like someone put a torch to it. We are trying to find out what type of weapon could do it. Hey! I thought you were going to bring two polar bears whose mother could have gotten kidnapped by Frostbite as well."

"I brought them," Jingle said. "They are in the sleigh. Poor things were so tuckered out they fell asleep before we even left Christmas Village."

Jingle and Caska made their way to the

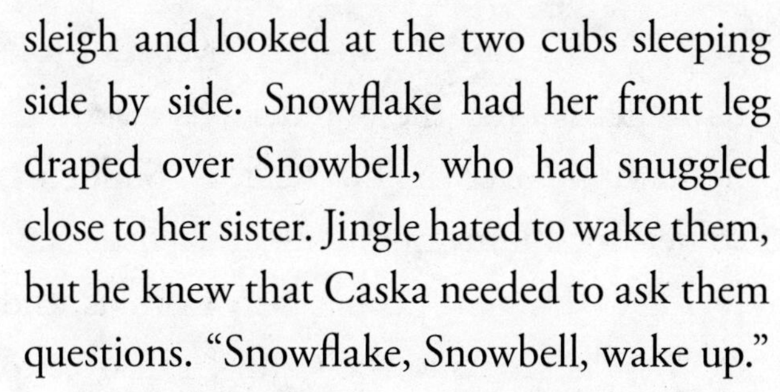

sleigh and looked at the two cubs sleeping side by side. Snowflake had her front leg draped over Snowbell, who had snuggled close to her sister. Jingle hated to wake them, but he knew that Caska needed to ask them questions. “Snowflake, Snowbell, wake up.”

Snowflake slowly awakened, but Snowbell continued to sleep deeply. “What’s up, Jingle?” Snowflake asked, rubbing her eyes with her paw.

“Caska, here, wants to ask you and your sister some questions about your mother.”

“Okay, but can we just let my sister rest? I can answer all the questions you may have.”

“It’s okay with me,” Caska said. “Could you tell me what happened from the beginning, until you were found by Jingle?”

“Well, Snowbell and I were playing in the snow, near some boulders. Our mom was cleaning out the den a few yards away when, all of a sudden, she heard the sound

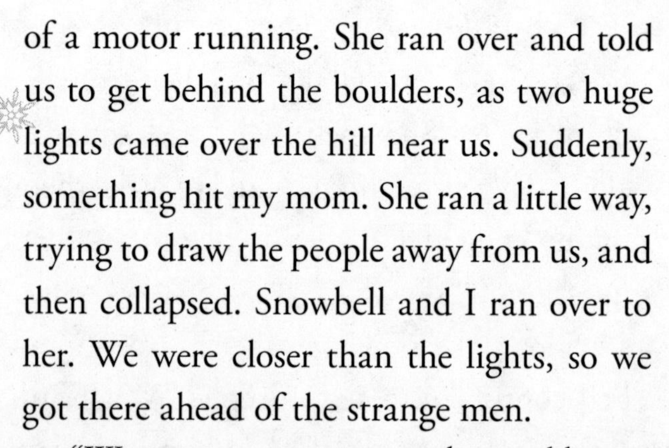

of a motor running. She ran over and told us to get behind the boulders, as two huge lights came over the hill near us. Suddenly, something hit my mom. She ran a little way, trying to draw the people away from us, and then collapsed. Snowbell and I ran over to her. We were closer than the lights, so we got there ahead of the strange men.

"We went over to our mother and began nudging her, trying to get her to wake up. She opened her eyes but was very drowsy. She made me promise that I would take care of Snowbell and that we would hide behind the boulders. She told me that no matter what happened to her, we were not to come out. Snowbell and I were both crying. I didn't want to leave Mom, but I knew I had to. I whispered, 'I love you,' in her ear and then I told her that we would find a way to set her free. Then she was silent, and no matter how much I nudged her,

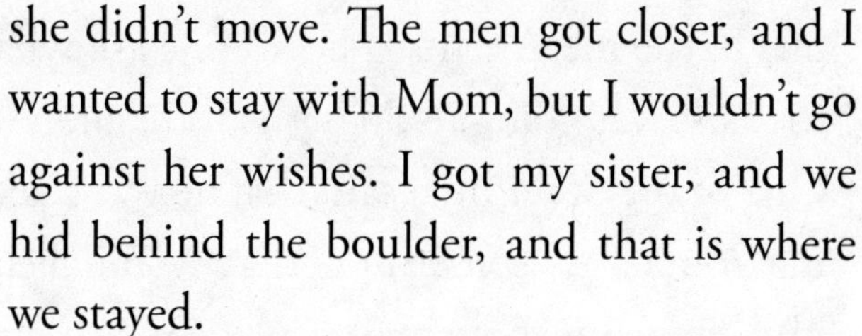

she didn't move. The men got closer, and I wanted to stay with Mom, but I wouldn't go against her wishes. I got my sister, and we hid behind the boulder, and that is where we stayed.

"I heard the men talking about how the boss would 'get a lot for this one from The Collector.' Then, one said that it would be even better if they could get the cubs. I figured that meant us. Well, anyway, they loaded our mother into the vehicle with the large lights, and moved out. Snowbell and I waited for a while, and then started to follow the tracks of the vehicle. We finally found them in a clearing, surrounded by trees. There was only one way in, and one way out. Snowbell and I snuck in at night and were able to find our mother. She was in a cage, off from the complex itself, and all alone. She was still asleep when we got there. I left Snowbell there and headed to

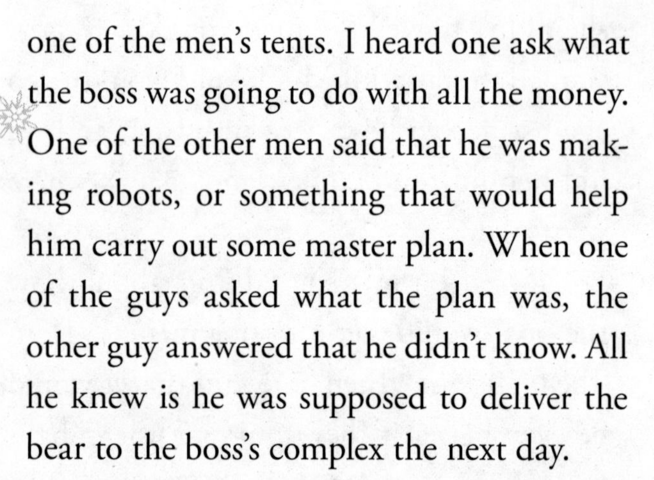

one of the men's tents. I heard one ask what the boss was going to do with all the money. One of the other men said that he was making robots, or something that would help him carry out some master plan. When one of the guys asked what the plan was, the other guy answered that he didn't know. All he knew is he was supposed to deliver the bear to the boss's complex the next day.

"Suddenly, one of the men saw me and shouted an alarm for all the men to come out, and they all tried to catch me. I ran and got Snowbell, and the two of us got out of there, as fast as we could. The men got in their vehicles and started to follow us. Snowbell and I were running and running. When we were about to give up, a huge blizzard came out of nowhere. It was so cold, and the snow was blowing around so much, we couldn't see where we were. The blizzard had also proved difficult for the men, because I

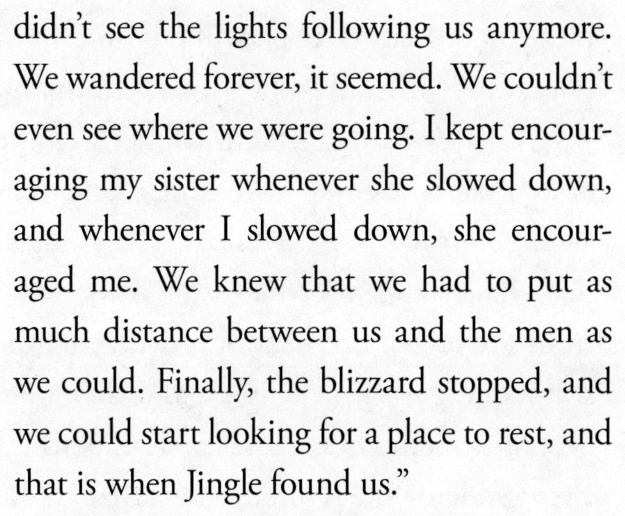

didn't see the lights following us anymore. We wandered forever, it seemed. We couldn't even see where we were going. I kept encouraging my sister whenever she slowed down, and whenever I slowed down, she encouraged me. We knew that we had to put as much distance between us and the men as we could. Finally, the blizzard stopped, and we could start looking for a place to rest, and that is when Jingle found us."

"Thank you, Snowflake. That helps a lot. I think the robots that the squirrel saw must have been the robots that you were talking about. Apparently, Frostbite is going to sell your mother to a man known as The Collector to make more money for his plan. Other than that, I don't know what his plan is," Caska said. "Well, I'm going to send some of the elves and reindeer out in every direction to try and find this big com-

plex you described. Each will take a Kringle phone and will call if they see anything."

Caska explained his instructions to the elves that had come with Jingle and sent them on their way, while Caska, Jingle, Snowflake, and Snowbell waited for word from the elves. The next day, everyone was still looking for the complex, and they were becoming anxious because it was Christmas Eve. Suddenly the Kringle phone that Caska was holding began to ring. Everyone there waited expectantly as Caska talked to the elf on the other end.

"I've found it. It's huge, and there are many robots guarding the complex. It is in Glacier Valley, and the mother polar bear is still here. I can see the reindeer. They are all tied in an enclosure and can't get away, but I don't see Santa," the elf on the other end of the phone said.

"Stay there. We will be there soon," Caska said.

Caska hung up and began giving orders to his security elves to load the sleighs and to prepare to embark for Frostbite's complex. As they were preparing to leave, in Glacier Valley, Fiona was coming face-to-face with her captor.

The Prisoners Meet

Fiona swayed as the vehicle holding her came to a stop. She felt like she had been sitting inside what appeared to be a trailer for days. Suddenly the two double doors at the end of the trailer opened letting bright light pour in. As Fiona's eyes adjusted to the light, she strained her ears to catch what was happening outside.

"Get that polar bear out of there," yelled an impatient voice. "We have to get ready

for our special guest who will be arriving any minute."

"She won't come out, Mr. Frostbite," said a mechanical voice.

"Then make her come out," said Frostbite, "but don't harm her in any way. I intend to get a good price for her."

Fiona had backed into the back of the trailer so if they came in they would have to contend with her huge claws and teeth. Suddenly a door opened behind her, and she felt a sudden sting in her hip. Fiona stumbled and finally fell asleep from the tranquilizer dart.

She woke up in a huge cage. Fiona looked around and realized she was in a compound of some kind. She saw several robots doing various tasks all around her. She saw the only man on the compound walking toward her cage. He was a tall, plain-looking man, with dirty brown hair, and cruel brown eyes.

"I see you are finally awake, and I bet you are wondering what you are doing here and what I intend to do with you," said the man. "My name is Frederick Frostbite, but most just call me Frostbite. As for you, there is a private collector who will pay handsomely for you. "

"Why are you doing this? Why do you have to be so cruel? Please just let me go. I am sure my cubs are cold and hungry, and I must get back to them," said Fiona.

"Oh my poor dear," said Frostbite coming to the bars of Fiona's cage, "you mistake me for someone who cares. My heart, my dear, is long since frozen from a lifetime of loneliness and sadness. As for your cubs you may as yet see them, for my men are searching for them. I can get a much better price for two adorable cubs."

Fiona came at the bars her teeth bared and her great paws reaching through the

bars trying to get a bite or claw into the cruel man. Frostbite had backed up quickly and stood there laughing as his robots raced over with spears, which they stuck through the holes in the bars forcing the polar bear back.

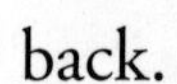

"Use another dart on her so we don't need to worry about her escaping while our guest arrives," said Frostbite as one of his robots aimed a gun at Fiona. As Fiona fell asleep she saw a large man in a red suit being yanked out of a truck.

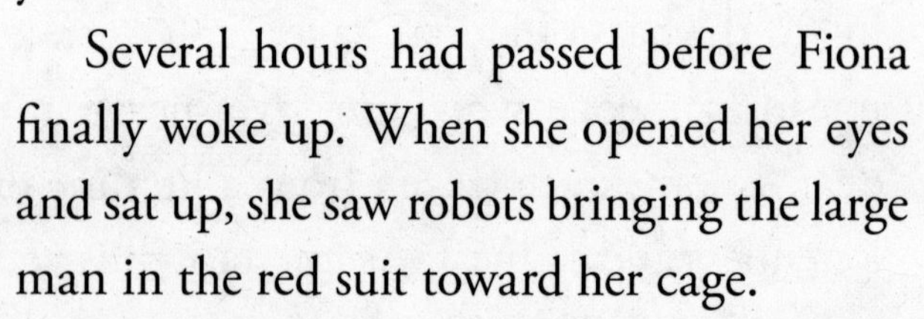

Several hours had passed before Fiona finally woke up. When she opened her eyes and sat up, she saw robots bringing the large man in the red suit toward her cage.

"Hi. I'm Santa Claus, but you can call me Nick," said Santa, once the robots that had thrown him in were gone.

"I'm Fiona," said the large polar bear.

"Do you have two little cubs that have

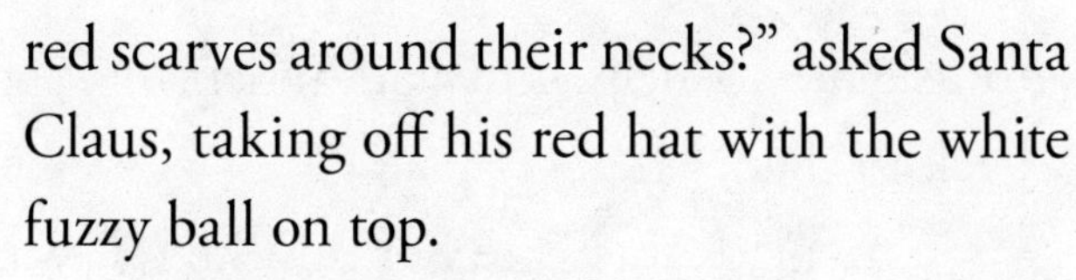

red scarves around their necks?" asked Santa Claus, taking off his red hat with the white fuzzy ball on top.

"Yes, why do you ask? They haven't been caught have they?"

"No, they weren't captured. I didn't mean to alarm you. They were found wandering near the North Pole, and my chief elf, Jingle, found them. I was on my way to see them, when I decided to check on my reindeer in the pasture. Then all of a sudden, these robots began herding the reindeer into a truck, and then one saw me and captured me too."

"Are my cubs okay?"

"Don't worry about your cubs. They are all right, and from what Jingle told me, they are very worried about you and are anxious to find you. In fact, the last time I heard, they were on their way to Christmas Village

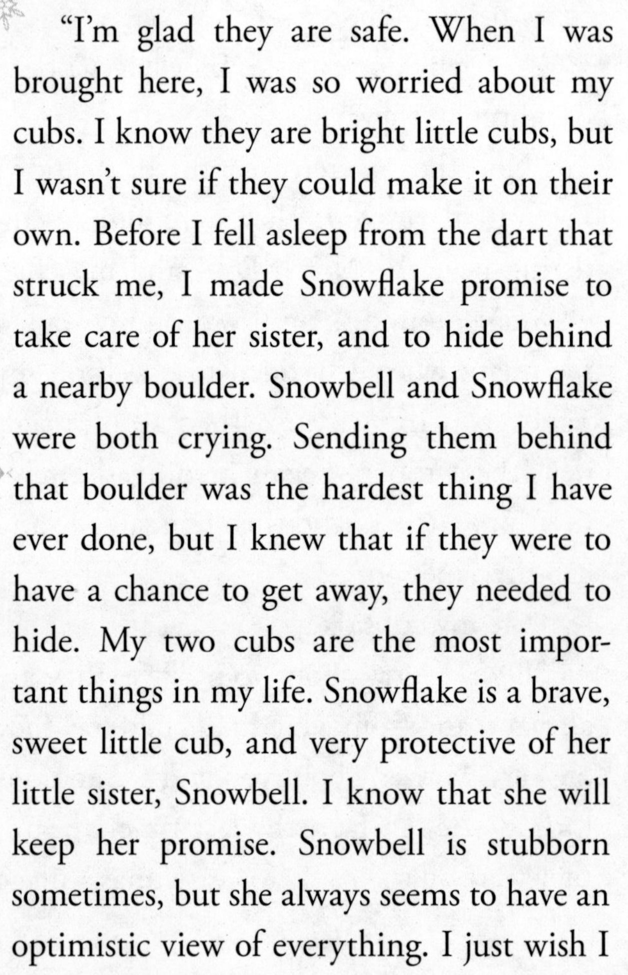

to ask me to help find you and bring you back to them."

"I'm glad they are safe. When I was brought here, I was so worried about my cubs. I know they are bright little cubs, but I wasn't sure if they could make it on their own. Before I fell asleep from the dart that struck me, I made Snowflake promise to take care of her sister, and to hide behind a nearby boulder. Snowbell and Snowflake were both crying. Sending them behind that boulder was the hardest thing I have ever done, but I knew that if they were to have a chance to get away, they needed to hide. My two cubs are the most important things in my life. Snowflake is a brave, sweet little cub, and very protective of her little sister, Snowbell. I know that she will keep her promise. Snowbell is stubborn sometimes, but she always seems to have an optimistic view of everything. I just wish I

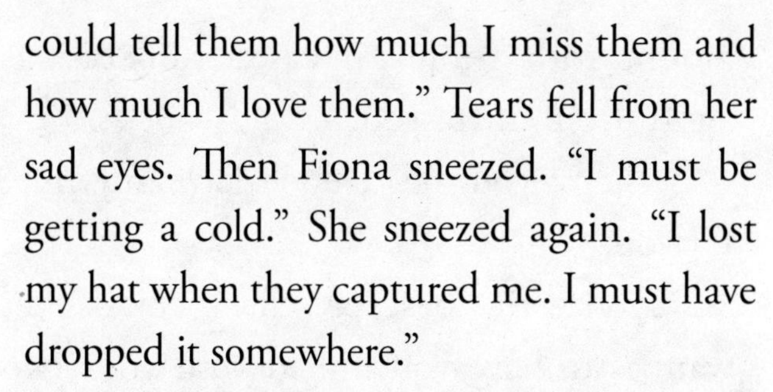

could tell them how much I miss them and how much I love them." Tears fell from her sad eyes. Then Fiona sneezed. "I must be getting a cold." She sneezed again. "I lost my hat when they captured me. I must have dropped it somewhere."

"Let me see. I know I put it here somewhere," said Santa, searching through the big pockets of his bright-red suit. "Ah, I found it."

Santa pulled out the prettiest hat Fiona had ever seen. It was red and had a white fur cuff around the opening, just like Santa's, and on the top there was a bright, gold star. "Here." Santa put the hat on Fiona's head. "This will keep your head warm, so hopefully, the cold won't get too bad."

"I couldn't take your hat," Fiona said, although she felt better already.

"Nonsense, it is an extra hat that I take

around with me, just in case. Think of it as a gift, from me to you."

"Thank you, but I don't have anything for you."

"Fiona, the best present I could ever want is to have you united with your two precious cubs by Christmas and I know that Jingle and Caska, who is my chief of security, will be mounting a search party as we speak. Don't worry, they'll find and rescue us. You'll have your cubs in your arms before you know it."

"I hope you're right, Nick. Do you know Mr. Frostbite, or what he wants with us?"

"When I was brought here, I saw Mr. Frostbite. He is an arch nemesis of mine, and he has tried to ruin Christmas on many occasions. The last time he attacked while we were delivering toys. He had invented a flying machine, but we were able to out-fly and outwit him. He said that he was going

to make sure that Christmas would never happen again. I tried to explain to him that he couldn't get rid of Christmas because all the children would be heartbroken when they woke up Christmas morning and found nothing under their tree. He said that was what he was planning on. He hated seeing all the happy children and cheerful smiles on Christmas, so he was going to do away with it. Rest assured though, Fiona, each time Frostbite has attempted something we have stopped him, and I am sure we will this time as well."

The two captives drifted off to sleep as a light snow began to fall, and as they dreamed, their rescuers were just arriving on the scene.

The Rescue

It was late afternoon by the time they arrived at the location of the complex. All the sleighs landed quietly on the hill overlooking Glacier Valley where the elf, who had found the complex, was waiting for them. The elf explained that there were at least forty-four robots around the complex and at least three that he could see around the cage that Santa and Snowflake and Snowbell's mother were imprisoned in. The reindeer were in a fenced-in area with a net over it so that they couldn't fly away.

The elf handed Caska a pair of binoculars to look at the security of the complex.

"Okay, elves, divide into seven groups," Caska said. He gave everybody the rescue plan he had devised. "Okay, Holly, take some of the elves over to that hill over there, and use the holly bombs. Merry, you take four other elves and some candy cane o'rangs and a candy cane key so you can free the reindeer. Jingle, you take a few elves and go free Santa and the cub's mother. Don't forget to take some tinsel. Dodger, you take the explodo presents and pass them out among the robots. Some of the elves and I will man the ornament launcher. Snowflake and Snowbell, you two will go with Boggle. Boggle, are you sure your plan will work?"

"I'm sure, boss. I tried it on Dodger last night."

"He did, boss, and boy, did it hurt. If anything will bring those robots down, it's

Boggle's secret weapon. It sure will boggle their computerized minds," said Dodger, as he gave Boggle a sneaky look. "Don't think I've let you off the hook for last night. I'll get you back when you least expect it."

The elves divided into their different groups and took their places. Holly took her group to the hill and set up the holly bombs. She ordered them to launch three holly bombs into a group of ten robots. The bombs were little metal contraptions in the shape of a holly leaf. The holly bombs were launched. Some hit the ground near a robot, while others hit the robots themselves. As soon as they made contact with an object, it exploded, sending little metal thorns everywhere. These thorns went through the metal material of the robots, and once inside, they exploded. The robots began falling, one by one.

Dodger took his group of elves and

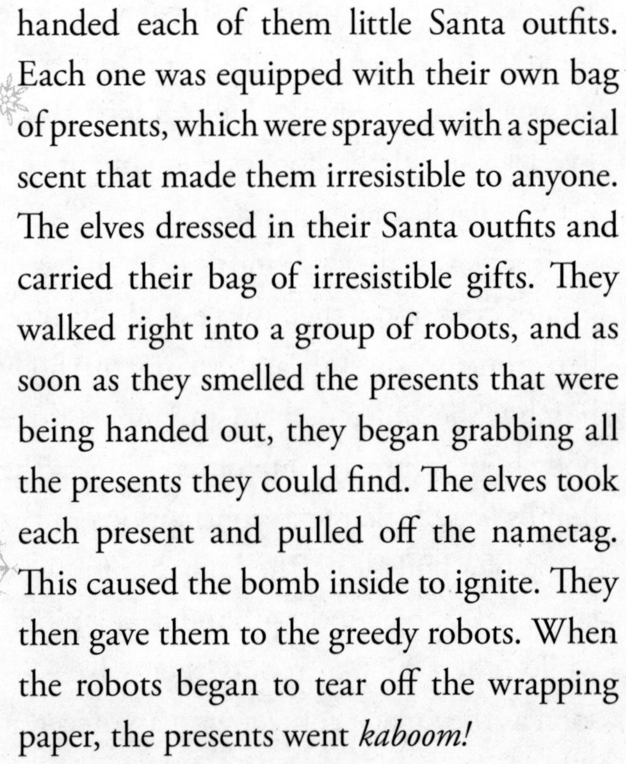

handed each of them little Santa outfits. Each one was equipped with their own bag of presents, which were sprayed with a special scent that made them irresistible to anyone. The elves dressed in their Santa outfits and carried their bag of irresistible gifts. They walked right into a group of robots, and as soon as they smelled the presents that were being handed out, they began grabbing all the presents they could find. The elves took each present and pulled off the nametag. This caused the bomb inside to ignite. They then gave them to the greedy robots. When the robots began to tear off the wrapping paper, the presents went *kaboom!*

Merry took her group over to where the reindeer were being held, and the four robots began to head toward the intruders. Merry and her group took the candy cane o'rangs, which were shaped like boomerangs. They threw these at the oncoming robots, hitting

their antennas and separating them from the main computer, which gave them their instructions. While the robots stood there, bewildered, not knowing what to do, Merry and her group took the candy cane key and unlocked the lock to the reindeers' enclosure. Jingle took his group and headed for the cage holding Santa and the female polar bear. The three robots that had gathered near the cage began heading for Jingle and his group. Caska, who had the Ornament Launcher on the hill with his group, gave the robots' coordinates to the elves and loaded a handful of ornaments into the launcher. Then he yelled, "Fire!" Six Christmas ornaments went flying through the air. These ornaments were of different sizes, and each contained a charge. These landed in front of the robots, and by the time they reached them, the ornaments exploded, creating a ditch that they were unable to get out of.

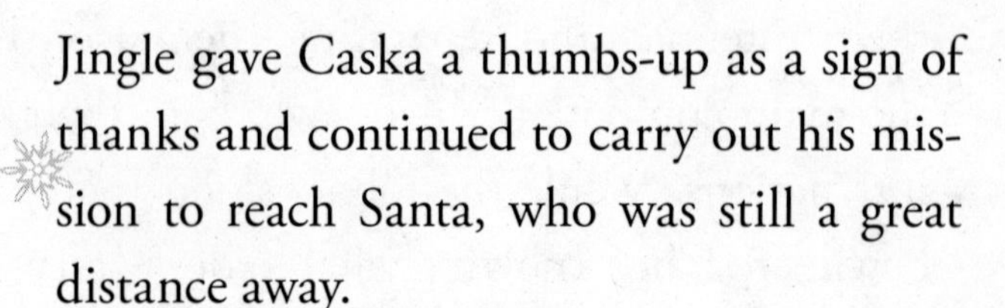

Jingle gave Caska a thumbs-up as a sign of thanks and continued to carry out his mission to reach Santa, who was still a great distance away.

As Jingle got closer and closer, Snowflake and Snowbell were having fun with Boggle and his group. Boggle took his group of elves, each with a bag of the secret weapons, and climbed into the trees in the woods.

"Snowflake and Snowbell, I want you to go up to one robot at a time and get them to chase after you. Lead them over here, and then I will knock them out," Boggle said.

"With what?" Snowflake asked noticing that Boggle had nothing but a big bag. Boggle reached in his bag and pulled out what looked like a hunk of fruitcake.

"Did Copernicus make those so they would knock the robots out?" Snowbell asked.

"No. My wife made them for the elves in

the village, but they are so hard, you can't cut them with a chain saw. I know. I tried. So I figured I could use them to knock out these robots. Just don't tell my wife. She is very proud of her fruitcakes."

"So that's your secret weapon," Snowflake said. She and Snowbell laughed as they headed off to find their first victim.

Snowflake and Snowbell each found a robot, which began chasing them. Once the robot was under the tree, an elf dropped the fruitcake on their metal head, knocking them out. It worked like a charm, but sadly for Boggle, not a fruitcake was scratched. The robots, however, would be nursing headaches for weeks to come.

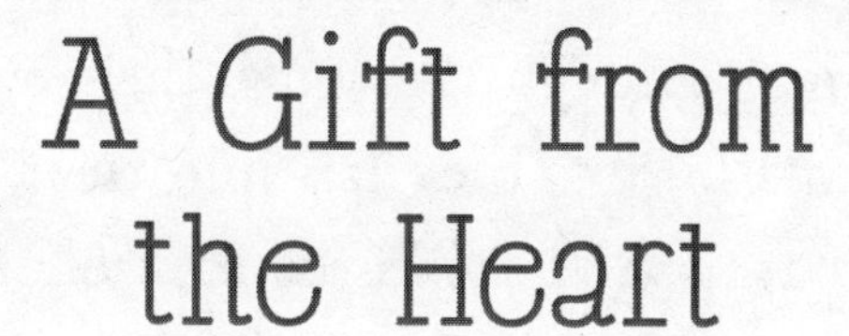

A Gift from the Heart

Jingle finally reached Santa and Fiona. Jingle took the tinsel and used it to slice through the metal bars. As soon as Fiona saw the elves, she immediately asked, “Where are Snowflake and Snowbell?”

“Don’t worry,” Jingle said. “They are with Boggle, knocking out robots with fruitcakes.”

Santa looked at Jingle curiously. “I’ll tell

you all about it later," Jingle said. "Right now, we have to get out of here."

Suddenly, Snowflake and Snowbell came running through the snow, their eyes full of tears of joy. They ran into their mom's open arms, and she kissed each one on the nose. "Snowflake, Snowbell, I love both of you so much. I thought I'd never see you again."Fiona looked over at Santa, who gave her a wink.

"Mom I told you I'd find you and rescue you. I love you, Mom, and I kept my promise," Snowflake said, looking from her mom to her little sister.

"I know you did, sweetheart, and I'm very proud of you."

"I did everything Snowflake told me to do. Well, most of it anyway," Snowbell said, not wanting to be left out.

"I'm very proud of you too, Snowbell," Fiona gave her youngest cub a great big hug.

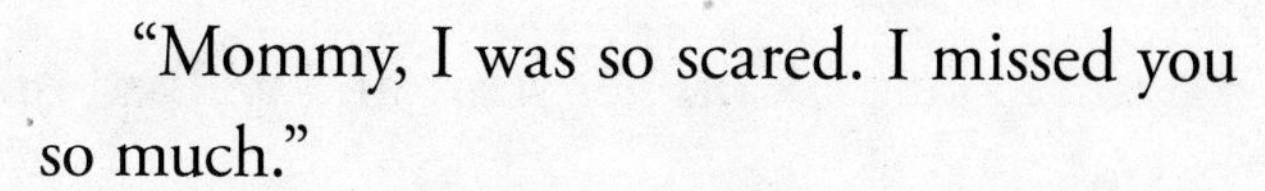

"Mommy, I was so scared. I missed you so much."

"Well, come on, we'd better get going," Santa said.

When they had all turned around to go, there, blocking their way, was none other than Frostbite. He was a very tall and plain-looking man, with dirty brown hair and angry brown eyes. Snowflake saw loneliness in his eyes, making her feel sorry that someone could be so lonely and angry at Christmas time.

"Nobody is going anywhere, especially you, Santa, and that polar bear," Frostbite said.

Frostbite looked miserable. *He looks like he has never received a present in his life,* Snowflake thought. *What could I give him?* she wondered. She didn't have anything but the scarf that her mother had given her.

Snowflake took off her scarf and walked up to him.

"Excuse me, Mr. Frostbite, my mom gave me this scarf, and now I want you to have it. Merry Christmas," Snowflake said.

Frostbite looked down at this little polar bear that was giving him her most precious belonging. His heart, which had been hardened by years of being left out of Christmas events, began to swell with Christmas spirit. He shouldn't be stopping Christmas, because it was a time for giving, and for hope and happiness. "Thank you, little polar bear, and Merry Christmas to all of you. I am very sorry for putting you all through such a horrible time. Will you please forgive me?" said Frostbite. "I guess I just figured that, since I had never had a good Christmas, or anyone to share it with, that no one should have Christmas either. However, this sweet little polar bear has shown me, with her gift of the heart, that Christmas is not about gifts. Christmas is a time for spending time with friends and family, and gifts from the heart are the best of all."

"Ho! Ho! That's okay, Frostbite. Everyone makes mistakes once in a while. I'm sure that everyone understands you and forgives you," Santa said.

Suddenly, an alarm went off, and Jingle looked at the watch on his wrist. "Santa, what are we going to do? It is already Christmas Eve night. We aren't going to be able to get back to Christmas Village, pack the sleigh, and take off in time for you to make the trip to all the children's houses," said Jingle anxiously.

"If you don't mind, I have a suggestion," Frostbite said. "I can drive all the elves, the polar bear family, and extra reindeer to Christmas Village. Santa can harness the

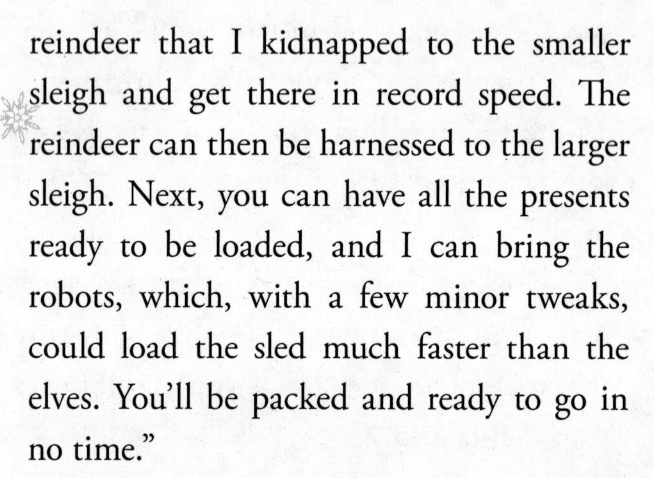

reindeer that I kidnapped to the smaller sleigh and get there in record speed. The reindeer can then be harnessed to the larger sleigh. Next, you can have all the presents ready to be loaded, and I can bring the robots, which, with a few minor tweaks, could load the sled much faster than the elves. You'll be packed and ready to go in no time."

"That sounds very good," Santa said. "Jingle, make the arrangements, and let's get this show on the road."

The elves were given instructions and were soon ready to head for Christmas Village. Santa and the reindeer took off and arrived at the village before Frostbite's vehicles.

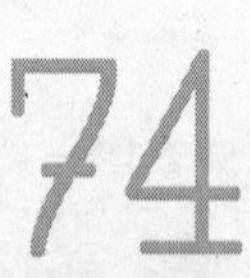

DANCER
DASHER

Christmas Is Saved

Once Frostbite arrived, he immediately fixed the robots, with the help of Dodger. As the elves harnessed the reindeer to the large red sled, they watched in amazement as the robots quickly loaded the sleigh. Suddenly, one of the robots went nuts and started going after Boggle.

"Someone, get this hunk of metal away from me!" Boggle yelled, running around and trying to stay ahead of the robot. Boggle

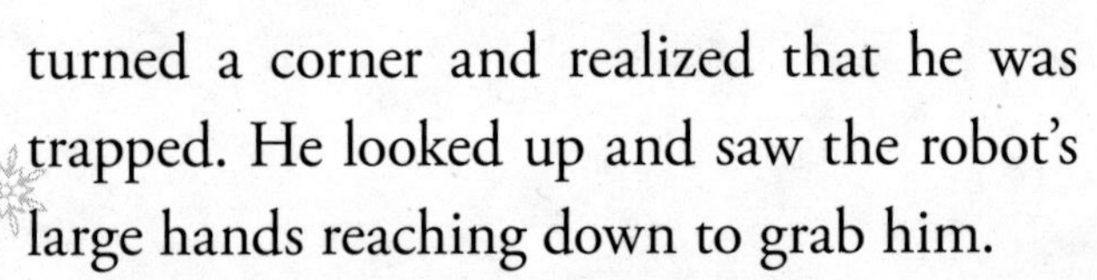

turned a corner and realized that he was trapped. He looked up and saw the robot's large hands reaching down to grab him.

"Hey, is someone going to help me here?" The hand finally caught him by the foot, and as he hung upside down, struggling to get away, he looked down at the robot's feet. Dodger stood, leaning against the robot with a remote control in his hand, laughing hysterically. When Boggle saw this he began screaming, "When I get down, I'm going to get you Dodger."

Everyone laughed. Even Santa laughed; his tummy shook like a bowl of jelly. Then Santa climbed on his sled and took the reins from an elf. "Okay, guys, let's get going. We have a lot of time to make up for," Santa said as the reindeer began to run toward the cliff. As they got closer to the end, Santa began to call them by name, "Now Dasher! Now, Dancer! Now, Prancer and Vixen!

On, Comet! On, Cupid! On, Donner, and Blitzen!"

As he flew across the sky, he yelled to the people below, "Merry Christmas to all of you."

Snowflake, Snowbell, and their mother, Fiona, finally arrived home in the morning, with the help of Jingle. Fiona hung up her red hat, with the star on top, on a coat rack. She began to prepare Christmas dinner ahead of time, because she had invited Jingle, and Snowflake had invited a surprised Frostbite to Christmas dinner.

Snowflake and Snowbell went to the tree and saw that Santa had already been there. There were thousands of presents under the tree.

"Mom! Santa has already been here. Can we open our presents now?" asked Snowflake and Snowbell, in unison.

"All right," said Fiona, going to the tree

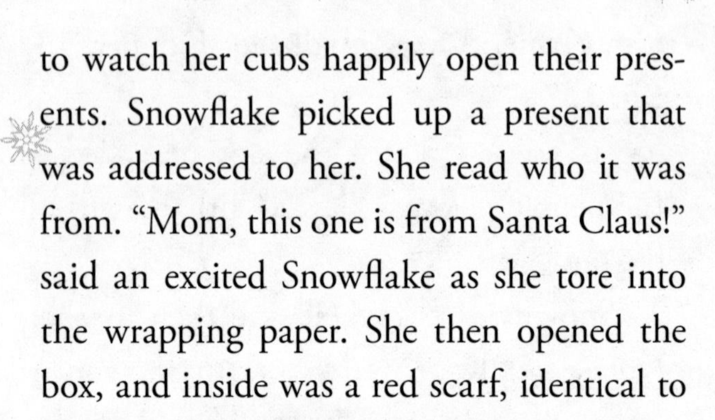

to watch her cubs happily open their presents. Snowflake picked up a present that was addressed to her. She read who it was from. "Mom, this one is from Santa Claus!" said an excited Snowflake as she tore into the wrapping paper. She then opened the box, and inside was a red scarf, identical to the one she had given to Frostbite.

There was also a note inside, and it said,

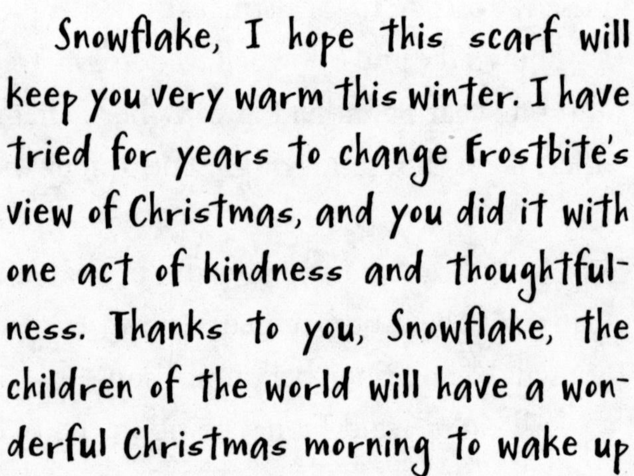

Snowflake, I hope this scarf will keep you very warm this winter. I have tried for years to change Frostbite's view of Christmas, and you did it with one act of kindness and thoughtfulness. Thanks to you, Snowflake, the children of the world will have a wonderful Christmas morning to wake up

to. Merry Christmas, Snowflake, and congratulations on getting your family back in time for Christmas. I'm glad I could help.

Your Friend,
Santa

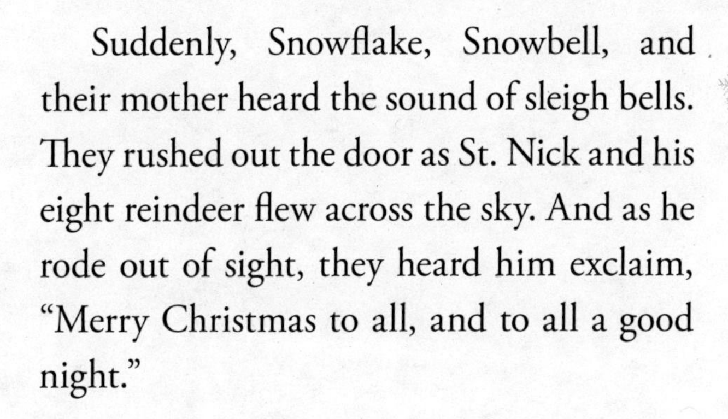

Suddenly, Snowflake, Snowbell, and their mother heard the sound of sleigh bells. They rushed out the door as St. Nick and his eight reindeer flew across the sky. And as he rode out of sight, they heard him exclaim, "Merry Christmas to all, and to all a good night."

listen|imagine|view|experience

AUDIO BOOK DOWNLOAD INCLUDED WITH THIS BOOK!

In your hands you hold a complete digital entertainment package. In addition to the paper version, you receive a free download of the audio version of this book. Simply use the code listed below when visiting our website. Once downloaded to your computer, you can listen to the book through your computer's speakers, burn it to an audio CD or save the file to your portable music device (such as Apple's popular iPod) and listen on the go!

How to get your free audio book digital download:

1. Visit www.tatepublishing.com and click on the e|LIVE logo on the home page.
2. Enter the following coupon code:
   ae99-6210-6034-887b-b170-5641-8da3-912c
3. Download the audio book from your e|LIVE digital locker and begin enjoying your new digital entertainment package today!